Santa is coming to

Hollywood

Written by Steve Smallman
Illustrated by Robert Dunn and Liberum Donum studio
Designed by Sarah Allen

Copyright © Hometown World Ltd. 2015

Published by Sourcebooks Jabberwocky, an imprint of Sourcebooks, Inc.
P.O. Box 4410, Naperville, Illinois 60567-4410
(630) 961-3900
Fax: (630) 961-2168
www.jabberwockykids.com

Library of Congress Cataloging-in-Publication data is on file with the publisher.

Source of Production: Leo Paper Products, Guangdong Province, China
Date of Production: May 2015
Run Number: HTW_PO100315
Printed and bound in China
10 9 8 7 6 5 4 3 2 1

Santa is coming to Hollywood

Written by Steve Smallman
Illustrated by Robert Dunn and Liberum Donum studio

sourcebooks
jabberwocky

"Well?"

boomed Santa. "Have all the children from **Hollywood** been good this year?"

"Well...uh...mostly," answered the little old elf, as he bustled across the busy workshop to Santa's desk.

Santa peered down at the elf from behind the tall, teetering piles of letters that the children of Hollywood had sent him.

"Mostly?" asked Santa, looking over the top of his glasses.

"Yes...but they've all been **especially** good in the last few days!" said the elf.

"Jolly good!" chuckled Santa,
"Then we'd better get their presents loaded up!"

Even though the sack of presents was

really, really big

and the elves were **really, really** small,

they seemed to have no trouble loading it onto Santa's sleigh.
Though how they managed to fit such a big sack into one little sleigh
even they didn't know. But somehow they did.

"Splendid!" boomed Santa. "We're ready to go!"

"Er...not quite, Santa," said the little old elf. "One of our reindeer is missing!"

"Missing?

Which reindeer is missing?" asked Santa.

"The youngest one, Santa," said the elf. "It's his first flight tonight. I've called him and called him, but..."

Just then, a young reindeer strolled up, munching on a large carrot.

"Where have you been?"

asked Santa.

But the youngest reindeer was crunching so loudly that it was no wonder he hadn't heard the little old elf calling.

"Oh well, never mind," said Santa, giving the reindeer a little wink. He took out his Santa-nav and tapped in the coordinates for Hollywood. **"This will guide us to Hollywood in no time."**

Crunch!
Crunch!
Crunch!

With a flick of the reins and
a jerk of the harness, off they
went, racing through the sky.

"Ho, ho, ho!"
laughed Santa.

"We'll soon have these presents delivered to Tinseltown!"

Santa's sleigh flew through the starry night, heading south across the Arctic Ocean. On they flew in the wintry air, high over Canada. In the wink of an eye, the sleigh was flying above Reno and past Sequoia National Forest. The youngest reindeer was very excited. He had never been away from the North Pole before.

They had just crossed over San Gabriel Peak
when, suddenly, they ran into a thick fog.
Mist swirled around the sleigh.

They couldn't see a thing!

The youngest reindeer was getting a bit worried,
but Santa didn't seem concerned.

"In two miles..."

said the Santa-nav in a bossy lady's voice,

"...keep left at the next star."

"But, ma'am," Santa blustered, "I can't see any stars in all this fog!"
Soon they were

hopelessly lost!

Ding-dong!
Ding-dong!

Then, through the
foggy blanket, the
youngest reindeer heard
a faint, ringing sound.

Ding-dong!

He looked over at the old reindeer
with the red nose. But he had
his head down.

(Red nose...I wonder
who that could be?)

Ding-dong.

Ding-dong!

Ding-dong! Ding-dong!

There was that sound again, like church bells ringing. The youngest reindeer turned around to look at Santa. But Santa wasn't listening. He seemed to be arguing with a little box with buttons on it.

With a flick of the harness and a jerk of the reins, the youngest reindeer gave a sharp *tug* and headed off toward the sound of the bells, pulling Santa and his sleigh behind him!

"Whoa!"

cried Santa, pulling his hat straight. "What's going on?" Then, to his surprise, he heard the ringing sound.

"Well done, young reindeer!" he shouted cheerfully, "It must be the bells of United Methodist Church. Don't worry, children, Santa is coming!"

Then, suddenly...

CRUNCH!

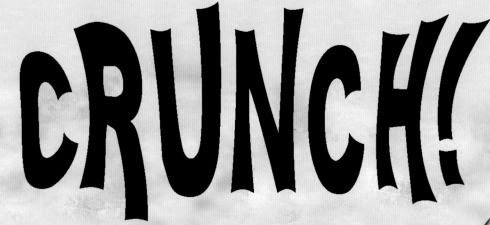

The sleigh hit something as it plummeted through the fog.

"You have arrived!"

said the Santa-nav unhelpfully.

Finally, when the fog had lifted, Santa discovered exactly where they were...

...stuck, right at the very top of the Christmas tree near Plummer Park!

"Everybody, PULL!"

The reindeer *pulled* with all their might until,
at last, with a screeching noise, the sleigh scraped
clear of the tree. Santa steered them safely over the
Hollywood Palladium, above the Zoo,
and down into Griffith Park.

Luckily, there was no real damage done, but the packages had all been jumbled up. Santa quickly sorted the presents into order again.

"All right," said Santa. "Thanks to this young reindeer I know where we are now. Don't worry, children,

Santa is coming!"

Santa drove his sleigh expertly from rooftop to rooftop all over Hollywood, popping in and out of chimneys as fast as he could go. *(pretty fast for a chubby fellow!)*

There were big chimneys in Hollywood Hills and small chimneys in Los Feliz. He squeezed down thin chimneys in West Hollywood and plummeted down fat chimneys in Larchmont.

The youngest reindeer was
amazed at how quickly they
went. Santa never seemed to get
tired at all! And it looked like the
children in Hollywood were going
to be very lucky this year!
But the youngest reindeer
was starting to feel a
bit weary and quite
hungry too!

He piled them under the Christmas trees
and carefully filled up the stockings
with surprises.

In house after house, Santa delved
inside his sack for packages of
every shape and size.

Santa took a little bite out of each cookie,
a tiny sip of milk, wiped his beard, and
popped the carrots into his sack.

In house after house, the good
children of Hollywood had left out
a plate of cookies, a small glass of milk,
and a big, crunchy carrot.

From Culver City to Pasadena, from Santa Monica to Silver Lake, from Universal City to Glendale, and ALL the places in between, Santa and his sleigh visited every house in Hollywood.

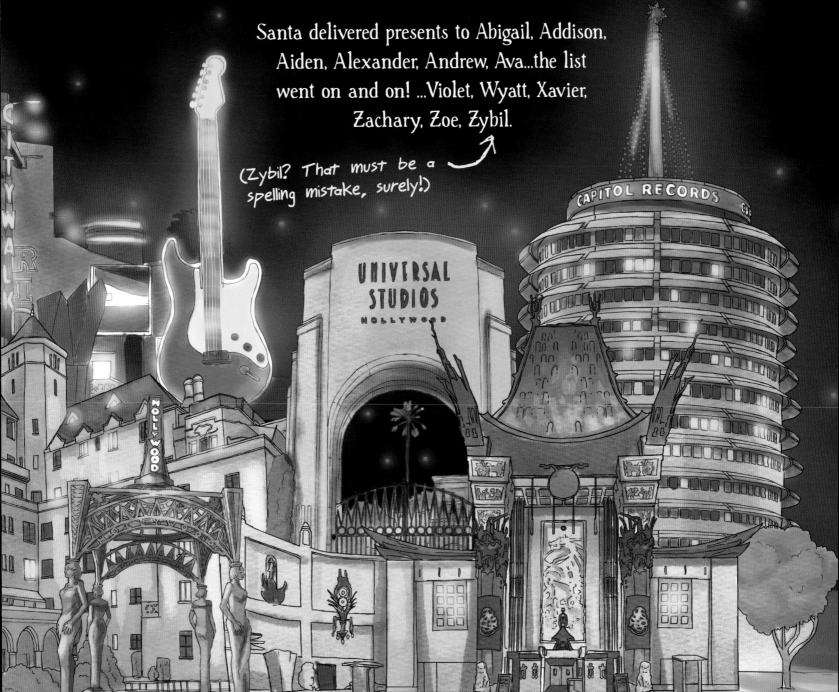

Santa delivered presents to Abigail, Addison, Aiden, Alexander, Andrew, Ava...the list went on and on! ...Violet, Wyatt, Xavier, Zachary, Zoe, Zybil.

(Zybil? That must be a spelling mistake, surely!)

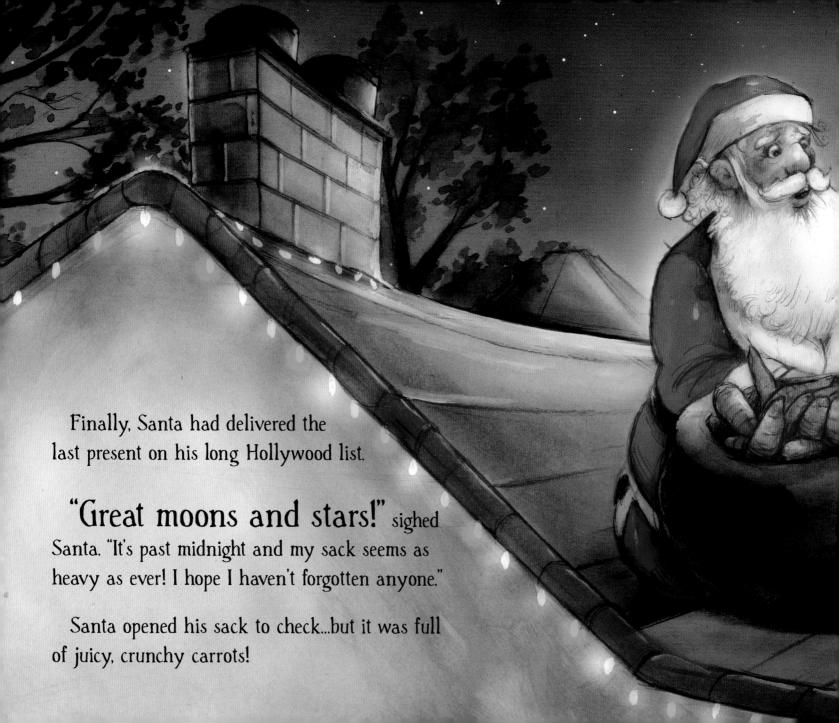

Finally, Santa had delivered the
last present on his long Hollywood list.

"Great moons and stars!" sighed
Santa. "It's past midnight and my sack seems as
heavy as ever! I hope I haven't forgotten anyone."

Santa opened his sack to check...but it was full
of juicy, crunchy carrots!

Santa divided the carrots among all the reindeer.
"Well done!" he said, patting the youngest reindeer gently on the nose.

But the youngest reindeer didn't hear him...
he was too busy munching!

Then it was time to set off for home. Santa reset his Santa-nav
once more to the North Pole, and soon they were speeding
past Sunset Boulevard, above the Dolby Theatre, and over
the Hollywood Bowl through the crisp, starry night.